This book belongs to

....

....

For Mia & Thiago

I hope you both always have the courage to
dance and go on many adventures together!

Published in the UK by Scholastic, 2024
1 London Bridge, London, SE1 9BG
Scholastic Ireland, 89E Lagan Road, Dublin Industrial Estate, Glasnevin, Dublin, D11 HP5F

SCHOLASTIC and associated logos are trademarks
and/or registered trademarks of Scholastic Inc.

Text © Gemma Atkinson, 2024
Illustrations by Lisa Hunt © Scholastic, 2024

Back cover: photograph of Gemma Atkinson by David Venni

ISBN 978 0702 32948 7

A CIP catalogue record for this book is available from the British Library.

Printed in Italy by LEGO.

Paper made from wood grown in sustainable
forests and other controlled sources.

1 3 5 7 9 10 8 6 4 2

www.scholastic.co.uk

DOGS DON'T
DANCE

WRITTEN BY

GEMMA ATKINSON

& ILLUSTRATED BY LISA HUNT

SCHOLASTIC

Meet ...

DAVE

Meet ...

DUSTY

Dusty and Dave do **EVERYTHING** together.

Well ... almost everything.
Dave **REALLY** wants to dance.

... But Dusty would rather dig.

Dave wants to TWIRL and SPIN,
TWIST and WHIRL.

... But Dusty would rather ZOOOOOM
around the garden.

The wise dogs in the park don't want to dance either.

The wise dogs say that Dave should stick to chewing
his owner's shoes, barking at the postman,
digging big holes and chasing cats.

Dave asks,
nervously.

He should stick to fetching **STICKS!**

At first, Dave doesn't let their words stop him.
He can't stop thinking about dancing and
how fun it looks. He goes off in search
of someone to dance with ...

"Do YOU want to dance?"
he asks the snail.

"NO!" says the
snail, rudely.

"I'm eating these leaves."

"Do you want to dance?"
he asks the bee.

BBBBbzzzzzZZZZZZZZZzzzzzzzzzzzzZZZZZZZZZZZZZzzzz

"Can't you see that I'm BUSY?" the bee replies.

Dave didn't think it would be THIS
hard to find someone to dance with.

"Do YOU want to dance?"

The cat hisses and dashes off without saying another word!

How **RUDE** thinks Dave, feeling a bit sorry for himself.

Dave decides to speak to Dusty again.
Maybe she'll say **YES** this time ... Dusty doesn't.

"Sorry Dave. I'm having too
much fun with this ball –
LOOK, it's so shiny and new.
I'm going to CHASE IT
and CHEW IT, until it

POPS!

... Do you want to try?"

"No ... I just REALLY
want to dance,"

says Dave.

He shuffles off with his tail between his legs.

To try and cheer her best friend up, Dusty rolls the ball to Dave.
But Dave doesn't notice **until it's too ... LATE.**

The ball rolls ... **and rolls ...**

...and **BOUNCES**

down the hill ... until it stops **KERTHUNK** by the base of a **HUGE** tree!

Dusty and Dave chase the ball. When they reach the tree, they cannot believe their eyes ...

The wise dogs' words echo in Dave's ears.
With so many creatures watching him,
Dave starts to feel shy and silly.

But the wise dogs said
I've got too many feet!

We've *all* got too many
feet. Just look at the bugs!
And don't get me started
on Mildred the millipede!

WOO-HOO! Go Dave!

Dave shakes his ears nervously.
Dusty and the other animals cheer him on.
Dave begins to feel more confident as the
music *thuds* and *thumps, bangs* and *booms*.

He lifts up his front legs.

He SLOWLY moves his paws.

He wags his tail.

Dave feels AMAZING.

DOGS CAN DANCE, TOO!

Dave feels so happy.

Losing himself
in the music,
Dave goes
WILD!

This time,
Dusty can't
help but
join in.

When Dusty and Dave stop to catch their breath,
they realize how late it must be.

"WHOOPS! Time to
get back to the park!"

They bid the party animals farewell.

Bye Dusty
and Dave!

KEEP DANCING!

See you SOOOOON.

When they get back to the park, Dave is still fizzing with excitement and joy. Dancing is **MORE** fun than he could have imagined.

Dave decides there's just one thing left to do.

His loud voice booms and echoes like a drum beat.

Dogs CAN DANCE!

DOGS...
CAN...
DO...
ANYTHING!

The wise dogs sit in
silence for a moment,
thinking carefully
about Dave's words.

They think about the things they love and the things they've been too scared to try.

They think about all of the things they **CAN** do ...

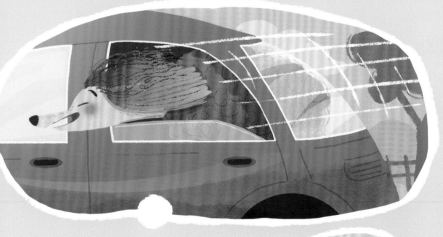

When it's time to go home,
Dusty turns to her best friend.

"I'm so proud of you, Dave.
You're the best dog I know."

They dance along as the sun
slowly dips behind the trees.

And when the stars sparkle in the night sky and Dave drifts off to sleep, he dreams about dancing with his friends and all the fun the future holds.

And Dusty dreams of the very same thing.

Meet **DAVE.**

Meet **DUSTY.**

They do **EVERYTHING TOGETHER** ...

And nothing can stop them!

If dogs can dance, so can you.
Why not try and learn some of their favourite moves?
GOOD NEWS – you don't need a waggy tail or paws to
perform them! Just mirror Dave's moves below.

THE DUST 'N' SLIDE:

1. Swipe your shoulder as though you are brushing dust off your clothes. Swipe, swipe.

2. Slide your foot out to the side, then slide your other foot to meet it.

3. Switch sides! Swipe the other shoulder as though you are brushing off dust again. Swipe, swipe.

4. Now slide your foot out to the side and then slide your other foot to meet it.

YOU'RE DANCING!

THE DOG STAR:

1. Start with your feet close together, arms down and wiggle your hips from side to side.

2. Jump in the air in a star-shape!

3. Repeat step 1, wiggling your hips from side to side.

4. With your arms wide, spin like a star in the night sky!

YOU'VE GOT IT!